SPIRIT LEVEL

Strange Tools & Story

Ellen Datlow

Kaaron Warren

Monica Carroll

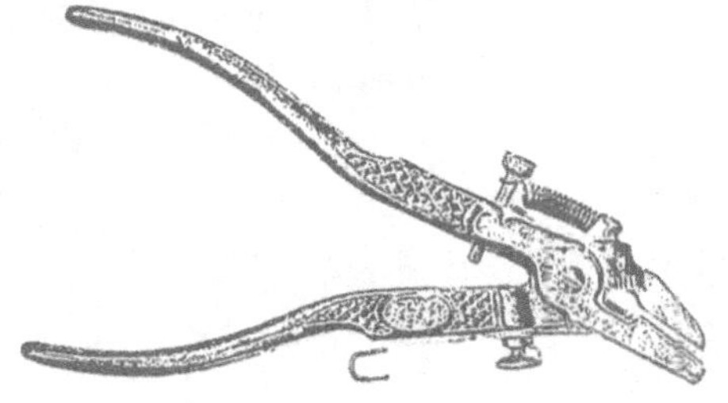

First published in 2025 by Dark Cave Press

National Library of Australia CIP
Title: Spirit Level: Strange Tools and Story/
Ellen Datlow (photographer)
Kaaron Warren (author)
Monica Carroll (designer)
ISBN: 978-0-6484036-7-8
Subjects: Horror fiction
          Tools – Fiction

SPIRIT LEVEL

Strange Tools & Story

Ellen Datlow

Kaaron Warren

Monica Carroll

CHAPTERS

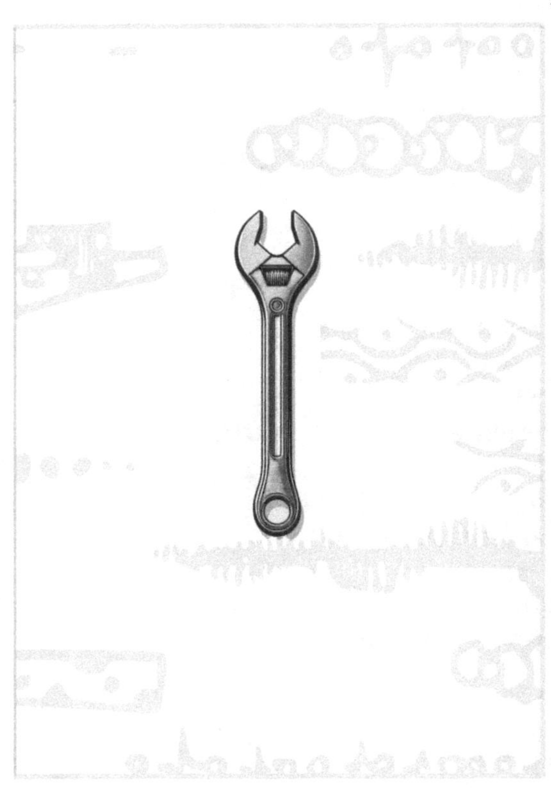

SHE FOUND IT UNDER

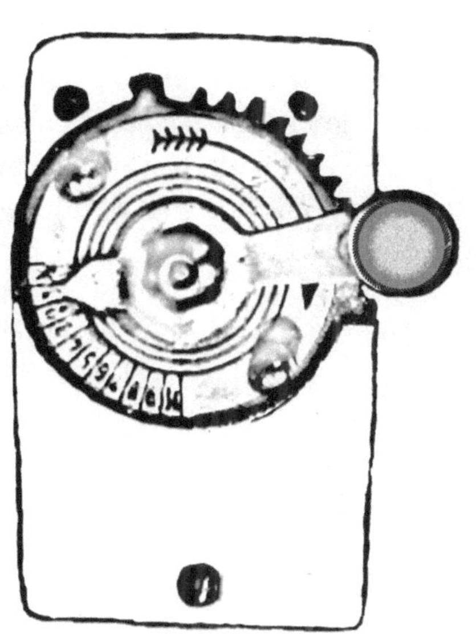

She found it under her grandfather's bed, hidden beneath a pair of pyjama pants that were stiff with dust. As she held it, the dial quivered and she wondered what it measured.

Her grandfather rattled, breath tearing his throat, and the dial lifted. She felt the tool warm in her palm.

One last breath and he was done.

Her grandfather had DNR tattooed on his chest, but she did resuscitate him momentarily over and over again, because watching the dial rise and fall made her feel a power she had not felt before.

At first he said, "No," and "Please," and "Don't," but then he said, "It's only right," and "This is just," and "True judgement" and she wondered what he'd used this tool for, that he thought he deserved to die and die and die again.

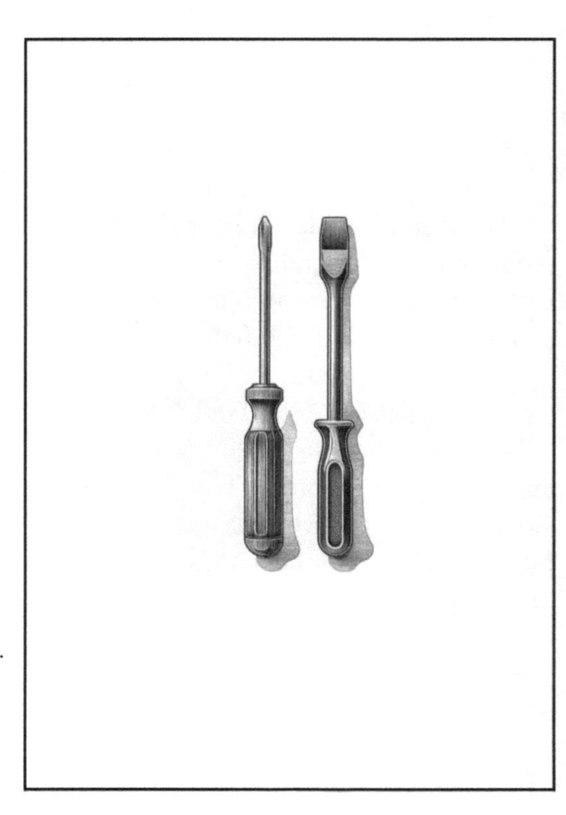

SOME ARE
BORN WITH

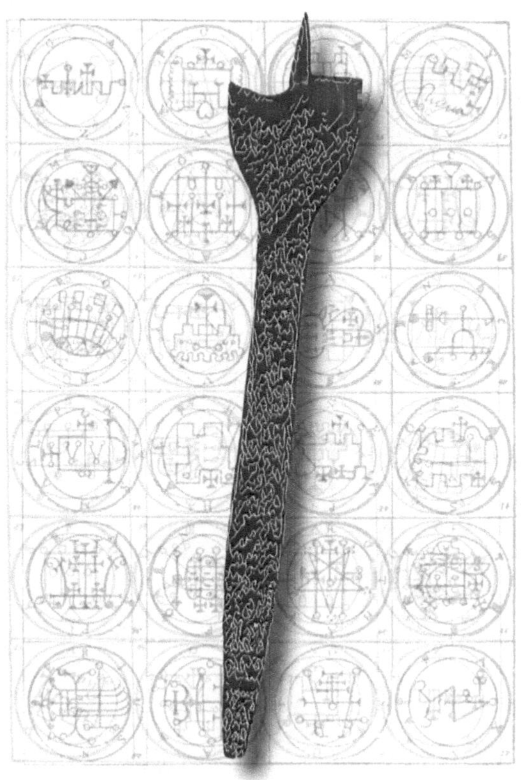

Some are born with a silver spoon; I was born with an iron tool. Half as long as me newborn, there are photos of me with my tiny hand resting on its length. Rust or something similar stains the sheet. Sharp at one end, sharper at the other, my father wrapped the tool in a bunny rug until I was old enough to be careful, or he tucked it under my mattress. That made him nervous, though. Really, he liked me to be in physical contact with the tool at all times.

He told me today the tool had killed a dozen witches. "Mothers, some call them," he said, and he began to train me for the day I might have to kill a witch myself.

I HAVE A COLLECTION

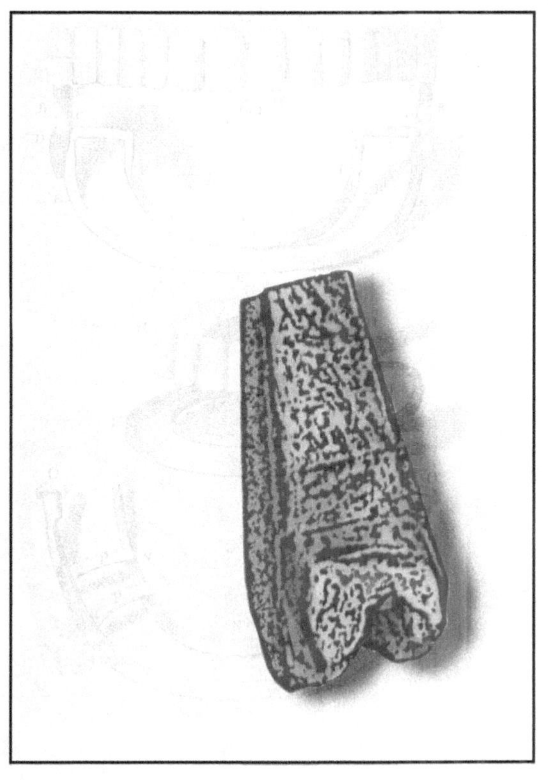

I have a collection of beautiful teeth. They aren't my own; I still have my baby teeth, set deep in my gums, unwilling to fall. Xrays show no adult ones waiting, none formed, and no one knows why.

So I take these teeth and I set them all in silver, because they are beautiful but imperfect. They show some decay, some decline like, perhaps, the people they came from. So I set them in silver and when I find the right dentist, he'll pull my baby teeth and settle these beautiful silver teeth in place.

In the meantime I'll practise my smile.

Because first impressions matter.

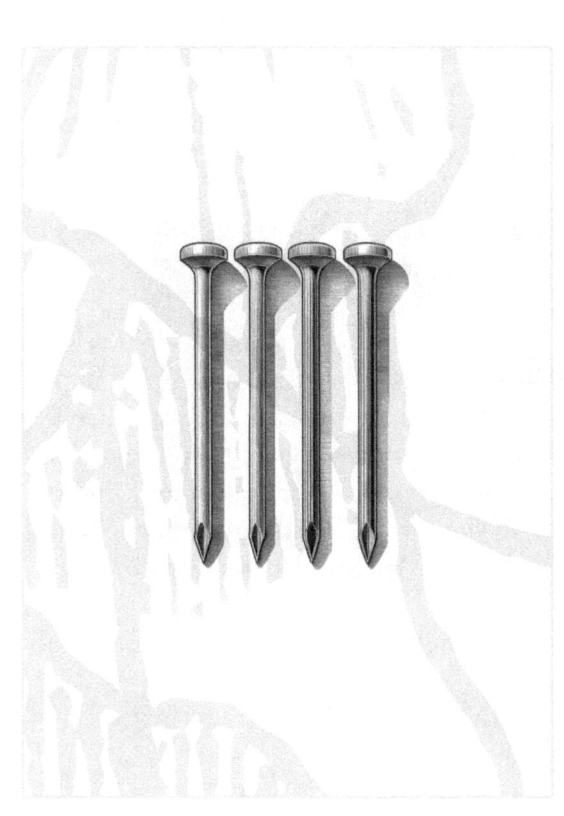

HE WAS A HANDSOME

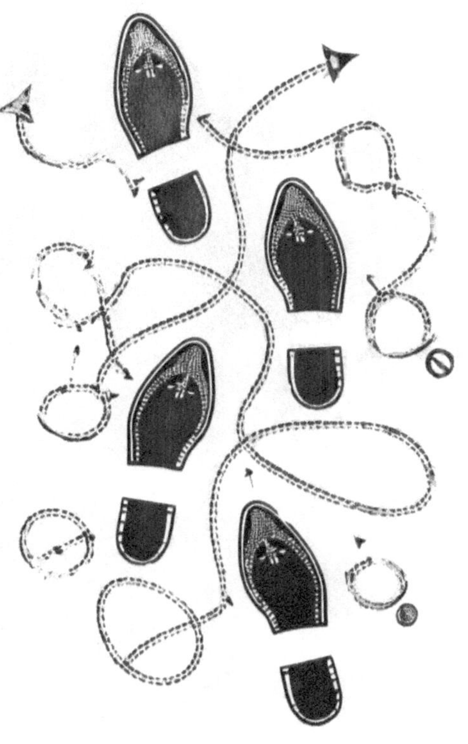

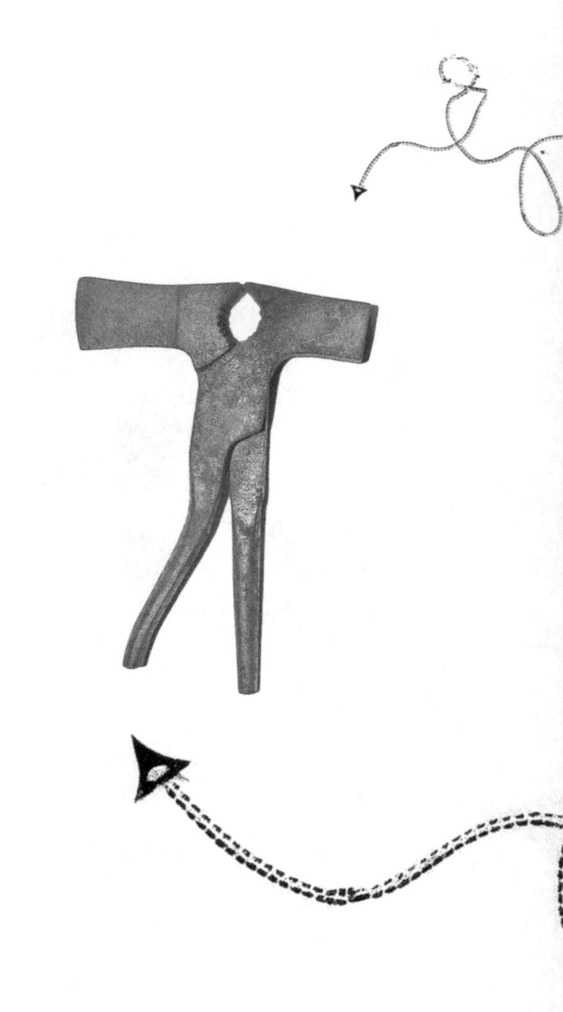

He was a handsome man. When he dan-
ced (traditional, wild, subtle or worshipful,
there was nothing he couldn't do) you'd
think he was a god. But you don't know
what's in a person until you bury them.
Leave them ten years. Then dig them up
and see what they've become.

A good man is rot and bone.

A bad man stays solid, hoping for a
second chance.

The god of dance was turned to iron,
frozen in a dance move that used to work
for him.

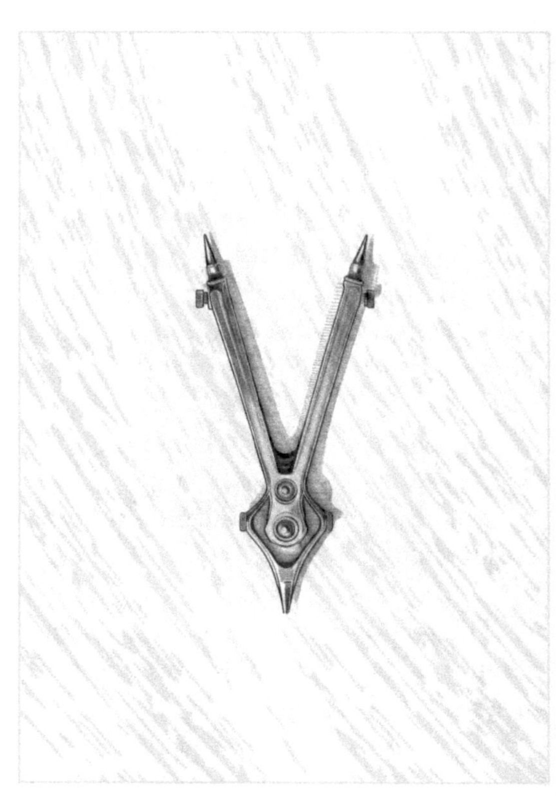

ONCE, WHEN I WAS

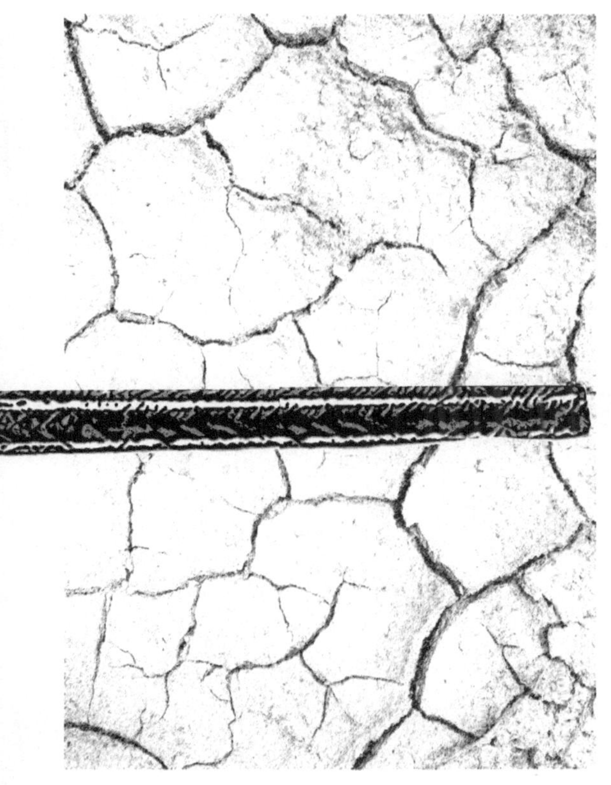

Once, when I was a kid, I turned on all the garden taps in my street. This was a long time ago, when Australia still had running water easy as that.

When we still had water.

I turned each one on only a trickle, so no one noticed until they stepped ankle-deep in the mud that water made.

Not the fastest practical joke, but a good one.

I wish I could laugh now, but my throat is so very dry. And all I can think about are those dripping taps, wasting water, decades ago. And in mind's eye I can see myself, lying in the mud, mouth open.

Drinking.

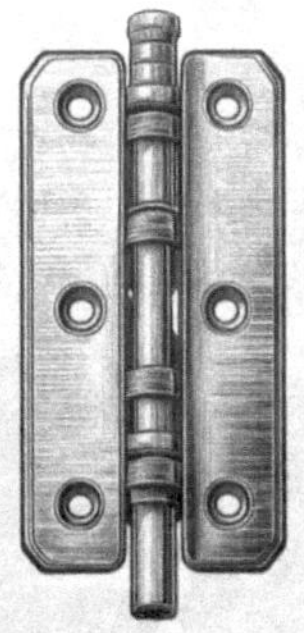

EDGAR FOUND
THE TOOL

Edgar found the tool buried in his backyard. An unusually heavy rain storm washed layers of dirt away, revealing many things: Bones buried by a long-ago dog, a child's forgotten toy, and this tool.

Edgar found it handle up and thought it was a small garden fork. The wood was notched and dented in parts, but still he dug around it, because most things are useful in one way or another.

He reached metal. A thick loop sat embedded in the handle, so not a fork. He tugged but it needed more digging out.

Even then, though.

Even when most of the loop was revealed it wouldn't tug loose and he didn't know why until, using all his strength (he was once a much stronger man. That, of all things, was still clear in his mind) he managed to pull it out of the ground.

Tangled around the curve of the loop was a thick, long lock of hair, with roots still attached.

He stared at the hole the tool left behind, knowing he would have to dig, but not wanting to remember whose head this hair once covered.

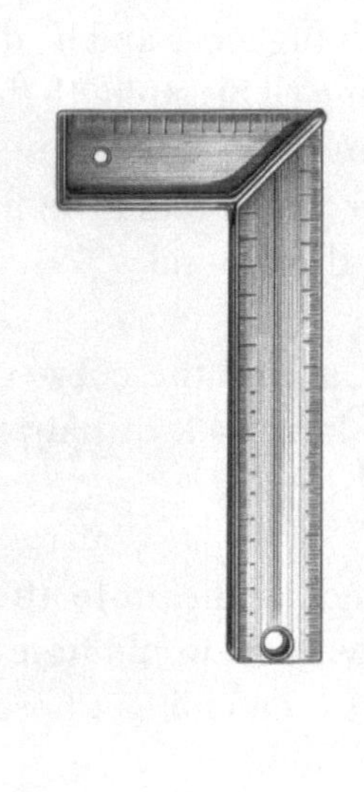

SHAKE THE EGG, APRIL

"Shake the egg," April would call out, curled up in her bed at night, and her mother would shake the perfect wooden egg. The two halves fitted together snug and neat and inside sat a silver thimble that had belonged to April's grandmother. April's mother shook the egg and the gentle rattle of the thimble on wood was a comfort. It meant her mother was close by. Within hearing distance.

They buried April's mother with that egg when she was killed by a sober driver, April's mother not sober, out looking for something she couldn't find at home. April herself closed her mother's fingers over that perfect wooden egg.

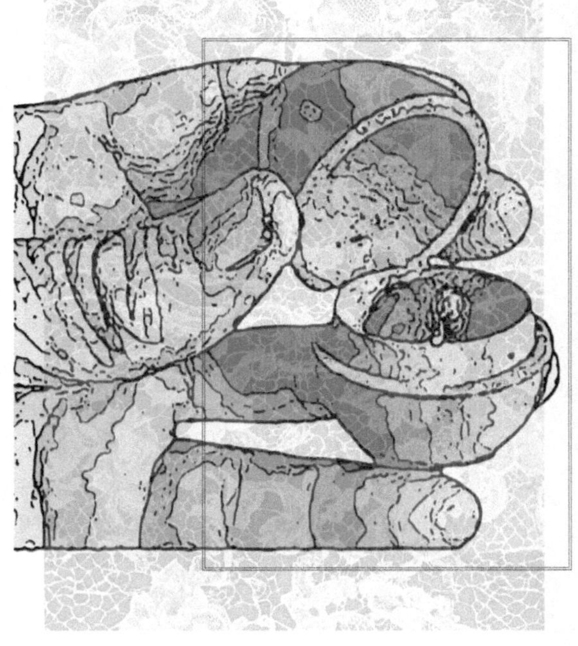

She thought she heard the rattle again, lying in a hospital bed with pneumonia.

And again, when a fire started from a faulty heater.

And then, finally, lying on the bathroom floor after a fall (old bones, poor reflexes) she said, "Shake the egg" and she heard the rattle of her mother calling her to comfort.

PRE-PAID HOUSING

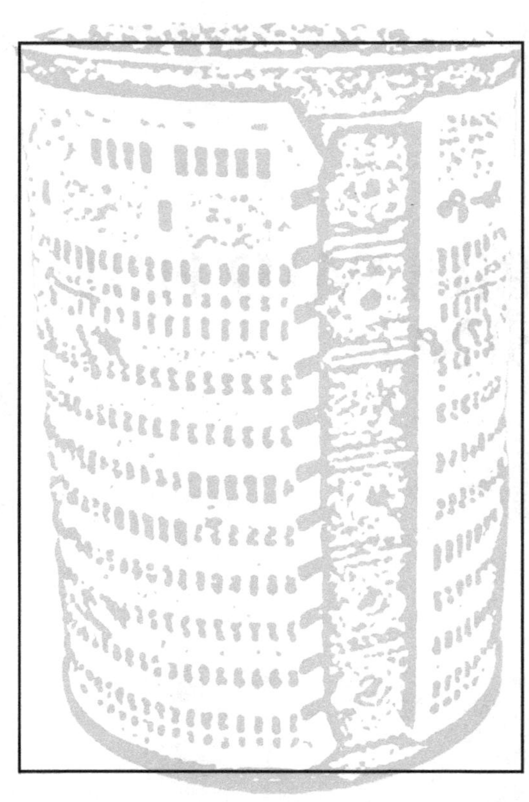

CASH
SPECIAL

In this house we all pull our weight. We know what our parents (grandparents, great-grandparents) gave up for us, paying week after week, year after year, sacrificing fancy dinners, second cars, holidays, so we could live in this house. The data tube that passed from generation to generation, kept track of the numbers, sits now in a glass box in the front hall, to remind us of what they did.

We are happy most days, with the cheer of our own children, the many rooms to explore, the beauty of the walls, the thickness of the carpet.

But other days, when in the distance we can hear the noise of strangers, the call of adventure, we wish, with all our hearts, that we could step outside just once.

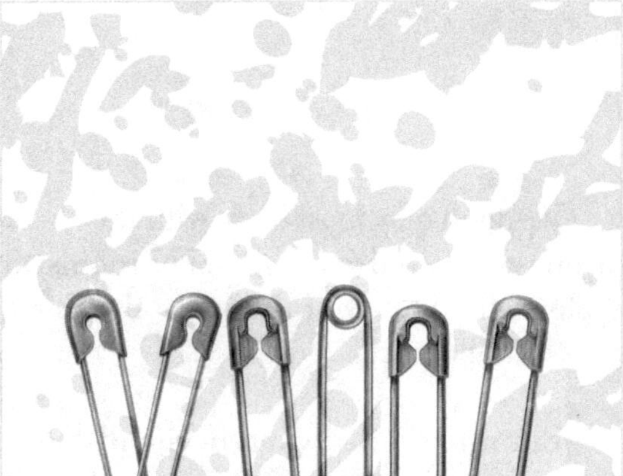

BIG MOUTH,
LOUD MOUTH

word
never
tongue
works
until I can taste blood.

worst is when the t too
hi stand on my
toes,

the words are in my head, now. But
y aren't listening, get
the speak.

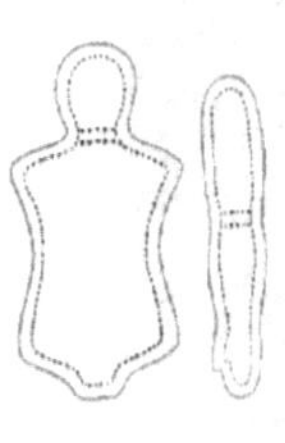
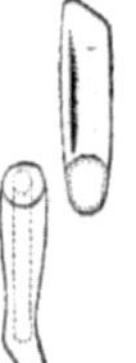

Big mouth, loud mouth, say a word out of place and in it goes. I've never been able to hold my tongue so I know the feel of wood in my cheeks. My tongue works at the groove, at the hole, until I can taste blood.

Worst is when they screw the thing too high on the wall and I have to stand on my toes, neck stretched.

All the words are in my head, now. But one day, when they aren't listening, I'll get the chance to speak.

THE LAST TOOL

卌 卌 卌 卌 卌 卌 卌
卌 卌 卌 卌 卌 卌 |||

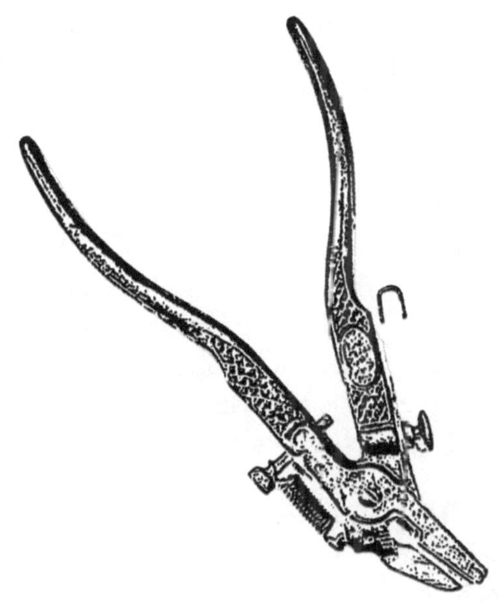

It was dark in his workroom but Ruedigen didn't notice. His eyes were used to the dark by now and if he worked in the shadows, perhaps they would forget he was there? Leave him be another year, or ten? Better to die here, at his bench, than where they wanted to send him.

He knew this was his last tool. "Are you finished?" they asked, and he said, "One more detail." He added a spring, a lever, a hook, another screw, feeling a familiar sense of excitement as he imagined it at work, pinching nostrils closed, pressing fingers flat.

"One more detail," he said, etching fine work into the handles. He tested them. They opened smoothly, closed with a satisfying snick.

"You can bring the tool," they said, surprisingly gently. "No reason why not."

So they walked out, Ruedigen blinking in the sunlight, and he saw that he had not been forgotten at all. The crowd brandished his beautiful tools (the self-timer, the auger bit, the iron pliers, the gas valve, the button hook, so many more), some smiling, many angry at what he had wrought.

Those many cheered as they used his tools against him in a very public execution.

TOOLS &
WORDS

Good books have a history. The history of this book began with Ellen Datlow collecting and Kaaron Warren imagining. Two things they each do best.

Ellen and Kaaron's collaboration on this work began online where they discussed the process of collecting, history, and the stories held within material objects.

Ellen shared photographs of strange objects she had collected over many years. Without any background information or research, Kaaron wrote a micro-story for each object.

They stopped at ten as it felt like the right number. Object ten was, in fact, the very first object that started Ellen collecting.

She bought it at Covent Garden's Monday Antique Market.

About This Edition

Originally shared online, then published as a chapbook (Tool Tales, 2021, IFWG), these photographs and stories were reimagined as a limited edition artist's book published by Dark Cave Press (Spirit Level, 2025).

This trade edition preserves the essence of that collaboration, bringing these strange tools and their dark histories to a wider audience of readers.

About the objects

1. Camera self-timer
2. Centre bit for bit brace
3. Unknown objects
4. Multi-tool
5. Part of a champagne tap
6. Button hook
7. Darning egg with thimble
8. Program drum and card punch
9. Multi-tool
10. Saw set

About Dark Cave Press

Dark Cave Press follows the way of devotional making. Books and curiosities emerge from the cave made by hand, made to be held. Small runs, strange works. Not infinite but intimate. This is our way.

To discover other artifacts from the cave visit: darkcavepress.com.au

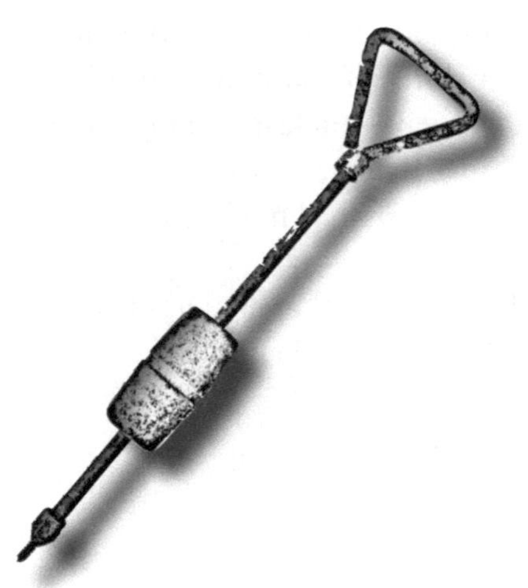

Your Turn: The Final Tool

We've saved one last tool for you. This one belongs to Kaaron Warren, and while she knows its purpose, we're keeping that secret. We're inviting you to look at this object with fresh eyes and imagine its dark history. What terrible purpose might it have served? What story does it whisper to you?

We'd love to read what nightmares this object inspires for you. Tell us:
@darkcavepress
hello@darkcavepress.com.au